The Halloween Pumpkin

Pamela Oldfield

Illustrated by Ferelith Eccles Williams

 CHILDRENS PRESS, CHICAGO

Library of Congress Cataloging in Publication Data

Oldfield, Pamela.
  The Halloween pumpkin.

  SUMMARY: The Halloween pumpkin goes about creating
havoc and scaring people. Then he meets a pig who is
not scared.
  [1.   Halloween—Fiction]   I.   Eccles-Williams,
Ferelith.   II.   Title.
PZ7.04538Hal   [E]   75-41346
ISBN 0-516-03582-7

American edition published 1976 by
Regensteiner Publishing Enterprises, Inc.
All rights reserved. Printed in the U.S.A.
Published simultaneously in Canada.

First published 1974 by Knight books and
Brockhampton Press Ltd, Salisbury Road, Leicester
Printed in Great Britain by Cox & Wyman Ltd,
London, Fakenham and Reading
Text copyright © 1974 Pamela Oldfield
Illustrations copyright © 1974 Brockhampton Press Ltd

"Halloween," said the old woman.
"It's a time for witches!
A time for goblins!
A pumpkin face will scare them."

In the garden was a big pumpkin.

She cut out two eyes. She cut out a nose.
She cut out a mouth full of sharp teeth.

Then she lit a candle stub and put it inside the pumpkin face. She pushed the face onto a stick.

"You will scare the witches and goblins," she said.

"And I will scare you!" roared the pumpkin. "OO-AH! OO-AH!"

It scared the old woman out of her wits.

"Mercy on us!" she cried, and took to
her heels.

"Ho hum! That was fun!" said the pumpkin. And off it went on its one wooden leg. Hop. Hop. Hop.

The pumpkin came to a bakery. The
baker was carrying a tray of new bread.
"OO-AH! OO-AH!" roared the pumpkin.

It scared the baker out of his wits.
"Mercy on us!" he cried. He dropped the
tray of bread and took to his heels.

"Ho hum! That was fun!" said the
pumpkin. And off it went on its one
wooden leg. Hop. Hop. Hop.

The pumpkin came to a fisherman. He
was fishing by the river.

"OO-AH! OO-AH!" roared the pumpkin.

It scared the fisherman out of his wits. "Mercy on us!" he cried. He fell into the water with a great splash.

"Ho hum! That was fun!" said the
pumpkin. And off it went on its one
wooden leg. Hop. Hop. Hop.

The pumpkin came to a farmer. The
farmer was carrying a sack of turnips.
"OO-AH! OO-AH!" roared the
pumpkin.

It scared the farmer out of his wits.
"Mercy on us!" he cried. He dropped the
sack of turnips and took to his heels.

"Ho hum! That was fun!" said the
pumpkin. And off it went on its one
wooden leg. Hop. Hop. Hop.

The farmer's wife was in the farmhouse. "My husband is late," she said. "The pig wants his supper."

The farmer's pig was in the sty. The pig was very hungry. "My supper is late. I want my turnips."

The pumpkin came to the pigsty.
"OO-AH! OO-AH!" roared the pumpkin.
But the pig wasn't scared out of his
wits. The pig was too hungry.

"Pumpkin for supper!" he said. And opened his mouth. Crunch. Crunch. Crunch.

"Ho hum! This is fun!" said the pig.
And he ate every bit. Even the candle
stub!

And that was the end of the Halloween pumpkin. Ho hum!